THE USBORNE INTERNET-LINKED

FIRST THOUSAND WORDS

IN ITALIAN

With Internet-linked pronunciation guide

Heather Amery

Illustrated by Stephen Cartwright

Edited by Nicole Irving and Mairi Mackinnon
Designed by Andy Griffin

Italian language consulatant: Giovanna Iannaco

Usborne Quicklinks: notes for parents and guardians

Please ensure that your children read and follow the internet safety
guidelines displayed on the Usborne Quicklinks Website.

The links in Usborne Quicklinks are regularly reviewed and updated.
However, the content of a website may change at any time, and Usborne
Publishing is not responsible for the content on any website other than its
own. We recommend that children are supervised while on the internet,
that they do not use internet chat rooms and that you use internet filtering
software to block unsuitable material. For more information, see the
Net Help area on the Usborne Quicklinks Website.

On every double page with pictures, there is a little
yellow duck to look for. Can you find it?

About this book

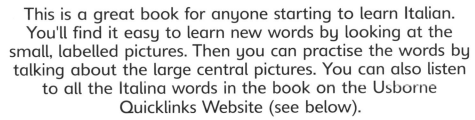

This is a great book for anyone starting to learn Italian. You'll find it easy to learn new words by looking at the small, labelled pictures. Then you can practise the words by talking about the large central pictures. You can also listen to all the Italina words in the book on the Usborne Quicklinks Website (see below).

Masculine and feminine words

When you look at Italina words for things such as "chair" or "man", you will see that they have **il**, **lo**, **la** or **l'** in front of them. This is because all Italian words for people and things are either masculine or feminine. **Il** or **lo** are the words for "the" in front of a masculine word and la is "the" in front of a feminine word.
You use **l'** in front of words that begin with "a", "e", "i", "o" or "u". In front of the words that are plural (more than one, such as "chairs" or "men"), the Italian word for "the" is **i** or **gli** for masculine words, and **le** for feminine words. All the labels in this book show words for things with **il**, **lo**, **la**, **l'**, **i**, **gli**, or **le**. Always learn them with this little word.

Looking at Italian words

A few Italian words have an accent on the last letter of the word. This is a sign written over the letter, and means that the last part of the word is stressed when it is spoken.

Hear the words on the internet

You can listen to all the words in this book, read by a native Italian speaker, on the Usborne Quicklinks Website. Just go to www.usborne-quicklinks.com and enter the keywords 1000 italian. There you can:
- listen to the first thousand words in Italian
- find links to other useful websites about Italy and the Italian language.

Your computer needs a sound card (almost all computers have these) and may also need a small program, called an audio player, such as RealPlayer® or Windows® Media Player. If you don't already have a copy, you can download one from the Usborne Quicklinks Website.

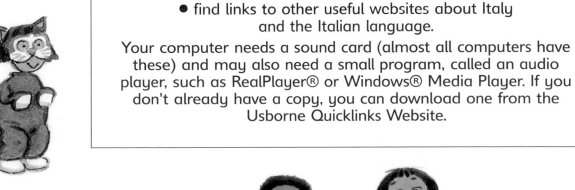

A casa

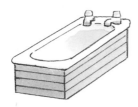
la vasca

il sapone

il rubinetto

la carta igienica

lo spazzolino

l'acqua

il water

la spugna

il lavandino

la doccia

l'asciugamano

il letto

Il bagno

Il soggiorno

il dentifricio

la radio

il cuscino

il Compact Disc

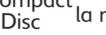
la moquette

il divano

 sedia

 il piumone

il pettine

il lenzuolo

il tappeto

 l'armadio

a camera lo letto

 il guanciale

 il cassettone

 lo specchio

la spazzola

 la lampada

L'ingresso

i poster

 l' attaccapanni

 il telefono

 adiatore

 la videocassetta

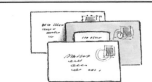 il giornale

 il tavolino

 le lettere

 le scale

5

La cucina

il frigorifero

i bicchieri

l'orologio

lo sgabello

i cucchiaini

l'interruttore

il detersivo

la chiave

la porta

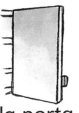
l'aspirapolvere

il lavello

le pentole

le forchette

il grembiule

l'asse da stiro

la spazzatura

6

  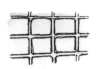

ollitore   i coltelli   lo spazzolone   lo straccio   le mattonelle   la scopa

la lavatrice

la paletta

il cassetto

i piattini

la padella

la cucina

i mestoli

i piatti

il ferro da stiro

l'armadietto

lo strofinaccio   le tazze   i fiammiferi   la spazzola   le scodelle

7

la carriola

l'alveare

la chiocciola

i mattoni

il piccione

la vanga

la coccinella

la pattumiera

i semi

il casotto

Il giardino

l'annaffiatoio

il verme

i fiori

l'annaffiatore

la zappa

la vespa

8

l'ape

la paletta

l'osso

la siepe

il forcone

il tosaerba

il sentiero

le foglie

l'albero

il fumo

il bruco

il rastrello

il nido

i ramoscelli

l'erba

la carrozzina

la scala

il falò

il tubo di gomma

la serra

9

Il laboratorio

la morsa

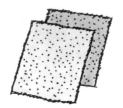

la carta vetrata

il trapano

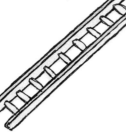

la scala

la sega

la segatura

il calendario

le viti

la cassetta
degli arnesi

il cacciavite

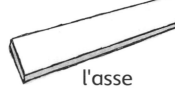

l'asse

i trucioli

il coltellino

10

le bullette

il ragno

i bulloni

i dadi

la ragnatela

la botte

la mosca

l'ascia

il metro

il martello

la lima

la vernice

la pialla

il legno

i chiodi

il piano di lavoro

i barattoli

11

La strada

il negozio

il buco

il bar

l'ambulanza

il marciapiede

l'antenna

il comignolo

il tetto

la scavatrice

l'albergo

l'autobus

l'uomo

la macchina
della polizia

le condutture

il martello
pneumatico

la scuola

il campo gio

il taxi

le strisce pedonali

la fabbrica

il camion

il semaforo

il cinema

il furgone

lo schiacciasassi

il rimorchio

la casa

il mercato

gli scalini

la motocicletta

bicicletta

l'autopompa

il vigile urbano

la macchina

la donna

il lampione

il palazzo

13

I giocattoli

il trenino

i dadi

il flauto dolce

il robot

i tamburi

la collana

la macchina
fotografica

le perline

le bambole

la chitarra

l'anello

la casa
delle bambole

l'armonica

il fischietto

le
costruzioni

il castello

il sottomarino

la tromba

le fre

l'arco

il paracadute

la barca

i colori per il viso

lo schiacciasassi

le maschere

la macchina da corsa

il cavallo a dondolo

il salvadanaio

le biglie

le marionette

il pianoforte

gli astronauti

la gru

la plastilina

il fucile

i soldatini

gli acquarelli

il razzo

la altalene

la buca di sabbia

il picnic

l'aquilone

il gelato

il cane

il cancello

il sentiero

la rana

lo scivolo

Il parco

la panchina

i girini

il lago

i rollerblades

il cespugli

16

 il bebé

 lo skateboard

 la terra

 il passeggino

 l'altalena a bilico

 i bambini

 il triciclo

 gli uccelli

 la cancellata

 la palla

 la barca

 lo spago

 la pozzanghera

 gli anatroccoli

 la corda per saltare

 gli alberi

l'aiuola

i cigni

il guinzaglio

le anatre

17

Lo zoo

il panda

le ali

l'aquila

l'ippopotamo

il pipistrello

la scimmia

il gorilla

le zampe

il canguro

l'iceberg

il pinguino

la coda

il lupo

le piume

il coccodrillo

l'orso

il pellicano

lo struzzo

il delfino

il leone

i leoncini

la giraffa

le corna

il cervo

il dromedario

la foca

l'orso polare

la tartaruga

la proboscide

il rinoceronte

l'elefante

il bisonte

il castoro

il serpente

la capra

la zebra

lo squalo

la balena

la tigre

il leopardo

19

I trasporti

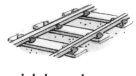
i binari

il locomotore

i respingenti

i vagoni

il macchinista

il treno merci

la pensilina

il controllore

la valigia

la biglietteria automatica

l'elicottero

La stazione ferroviaria

La stazione di servizio

i segnali

lo zaino

i fari

il motore

la ruota   la batte

20

l'aereo

l'hostess

la pista di atterraggio

la torre di controllo

L'aeroporto

lo steward

il pilota

l'autolavaggio

il portabagagli

la benzina

il carro attrezzi

Autolavaggio

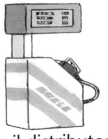
il distributore di benzina

autocisterna

la chiave inglese

il pneumatico

il cofano

l'olio

il mulino a vento

la mongolfiera

la farfalla

la lucertola

le pietre

la volpe

il ruscello

il cartello stradale

il riccio

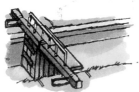

la chiusa

La campagna

la montagna

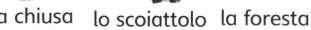

lo scoiattolo   la foresta

il tasso

il fiume

la strada

22

le tende

il canale

i ceppi

il villaggio

la falena

il ponte

la chiatta

la cascata

il gufo

la galleria

i volpacchiotti

la talpa

il pescatore

i massi

il rospo

il treno

la roulotte

la collina

23

il mucchio di fieno

il cane pastore

le anatre

gli agnelli

lo stagno

i pulcini

il fienile

il porcile

il toro

gli anatroccoli

il pollaio

24   il trattore

La fattoria

il gallo

le oche

l'autocisterna

il capannone

il fango

il carret

 gricoltore

 il campo

le galline

il vitello

la staccionata

la sella

 la stalla

 la mucca

 l'aratro

 il frutteto

 la scuderia

 i maialini

 la pastorella

 i tacchini

lo spaventapasseri

 il fieno

le pecore

 le balle di paglia

 il cavallo

 i maiali

 la casa colonica

25

la barca a vela

il mare

il remo

il faro

la paletta

il secchiello

la stella marina

il castello
di sabbia

l'ombrellone

la bandiera

il marinaio

Al mare

la conchiglia

il granchio

il gabbiano   l'isola

il motoscafo   lo sci nautic

26

le onde

il cappello da sole

la scogliera

la nave

la canoa

la fune

i ciottoli

le alghe

la rete

la pagaia

il peschereccio

le pinne

l'asino

il pesce

la sedia a sdraio

costume da bagno

la petroliera

la spiaggia

la barca a remi

27

le forbici

le addizioni

la gomma

il righello

le fotografie

i pennarelli

le puntine
da disegno

i colori

il bambino

la matita

A scuola

la lavagna

il banco

i libri

la penna

la colla

i gessetti

il diseg

28

il cestino della carta

l'insegnante

la scatola

la carta geografica

il pennello

il soffitto

la parete

il pavimento

il quaderno

l'alfabeto

la spilla

l'acquario

la carta

l'avvolgibile

il cavalletto

la maniglia della porta

la pianta

il mappamondo

la bambina

i pastelli

la lampada

a b c d e f g
h i j k l m n
o p q r s t u
v w x y z

a b c d e f g
h i j k l m n
o p q r s t u
v w x y z

29

l'infermiere

il cotone idrofilo

la medicina

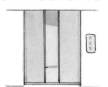
l'ascensore

la vestaglia

le grucce

il pillole

il vassoio

l'orologio

il termometro

L'ospedale

l'orsacchiotto

la me

la tenda

la tenda

il gesso

la fascia

la sedia a rotelle

il puzzle

la dottoressa

la siringa

30

Dal dottore

le pantofole

il computer

il cerotto

la banana

l'uva

il cestino

i giocattoli

la pera

la cartoline

il pannolino

il bastone

la sala d'aspetto

televisore

la camica da notte

il pigiama

l'arancia

i fazzoletti di carta

il fumetto

31

La festa

il palloncino

la cioccolata

la caramella

la finestra

i fuochi d'artificio

il nastro

la torta

la cannuccia

la candela

le decorazioni di carta

i giocattoli

nandarino

 il salame

 la musicassetta

 la salsiccia

 le patatine

 i costumi

 la ciliegia

 il succo di frutta

 il lampone

 la fragola

 la lampadina

 panino

 il burro

 il biscotto

il formaggio

 il pane

 la tovaglia

33

Il negozio

il pompelmo

la carota

il cavolfiore

il porro

il fungo

il cetriolo

il limone

il sedano

l'albicocca

il melone

la borsa della spes

FORMAGGI

FRUTTA E VERDURA

la cipolla

il cavolo

la pesca

la lattuga

i piselli

il pomo

34

e uova

 la susina

 la farina

 la bilancia

i barattoli

la carne

 l'ananas

 lo yogurt

 il cestino

 le bottiglie

 la borsa

 il borsellino

 i soldi

il cibo in scatola

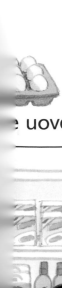

 e patate

 gli spinaci

 i fagiolini

 la cassa

 la zucca

 il carrello

I pasti

la colazione

il pranzo

l'uovo sodo

il caffè

l'uovo fritto

il pane tostato

la marmellata

la panna

il latte

i cereali

la cioccolata calda

lo zucchero

il miele

il sale

il pepe

il tè

la teiera

le frittelle

i panini

la cena

il prosciutto

la minestra

la frittata

l'insalata

le bacchette

l'hamburger

il pollo

il riso

il ketchup

gli spaghetti

il purè

la pizza

le patatine fritte

i dolci

Me stesso

la testa

i capelli

il viso

il braccio

il gomito

la pancia

le sopracciglia

l'occhio

il naso

la guancia

la bocca

le labbra

i denti

la lingua

il mento

le orecchie

il collo

le spalle

le dita dei piedi

il piede

la gamba

il ginocchio

il torace

la schiena

il sedere

la mano

il pollice

le dita della mar

38

vestiti

 i calzini

 le mutande

 la canottiera

 i pantaloni

 i jeans

 la maglietta

 la gonna

 la camicia

 la cravatta

 i pantaloncini

 la calzamaglia

 il vestito

 il maglione

 la felpa

 il cardigan

 la sciarpa

 il fazzoletto

 le scarpe da ginnastica

 le scarpe

 i sandali

 gli stivali di gomma

 i guanti

 la cintura

 la fibbia

 la cerniera lampo

 i lacci per le scarpe

 i bottoni

 le asole

le tasche

 il cappotto

 il giubbotto

 il berretto

 il cappello

I mestieri

il cuoco

l'attore   l'attrice

i cantanti

i ballerini

l'astronauta

il macellaio

i poliziotti

il falegname

il pompiere

l'artista

il giudice

i meccanici

il parrucchiere

la camionista

il conducente di autobus

la dentista

il subacqueo

il cameriere   la cameriera

il postino

l'imbianchino

la fornaia

La famiglia

il figlio
il fratello

la figlia
la sorella

la madre
la moglie

il padre
il marito

la zia   lo zio

il cugino

il nonno

la nonna

41

Le azioni

ridere

sorridere

piangere

pensare

ascoltare

acchiappare

lanciare

rompere

dipingere

scrivere

spaccare

tagliare

mangiare

parlare

scavare

portare

bere

fare

saltare

ballare

lavarsi

lavorare a maglia

camminare a carponi

42

giocare

guardare

arrampicarsi

prendere

saltare la corda

fare a botte

dormire

cucire

aspettare

cucinare

nascondersi

leggere

comprare

spingere

cantare

soffiare

tirare

spazzare

raccogliere

cadere

camminare

correre

stare seduti

43

I contrari

buono

cattivo

lontano

vicino

in cima

in fondo

freddo

caldo

bagnato

asciutto

sporco

pulito

sopra

sotto

grasso

magro

aperto

chiuso

piccolo

grande

pochi

molti

primo

ultimo

sinistra

44

fuori

dentro

facile

difficile

vuoto

pieno

morbido

duro

davanti

alto

lento

veloce

dietro

basso

lungo

corto

morto

vivo

scuro

chiaro

su

vecchio

destra

nuovo

giù

45

I giorni

martedì

giovedì

lunedì

mercoledì

venerdì

sabato

domenica

il calendario

la mattina

la sera

il sole

la notte

la luna

la stella

lo Spazio

il pianeta

l'astronave

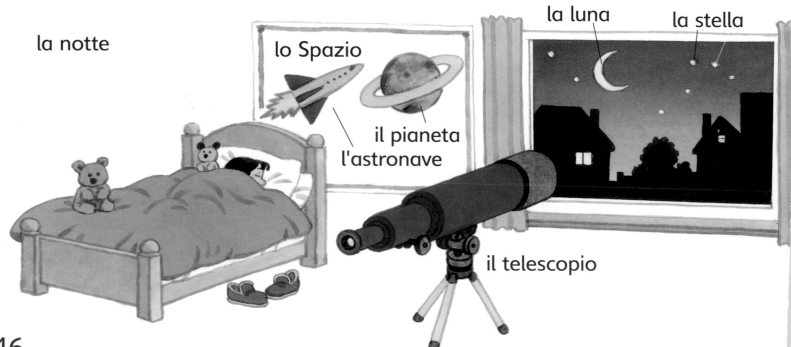

il telescopio

Giorni speciali

compleanno

il regalo

le candeline

il biglietto di auguri

la torta

la vacanza

matrimonio

la damigella d'onore

la sposa   lo sposo

la macchina fotografica

il fotografo

Natale

Babbo Natale

la slitta

l'albero di Natale

la renna

Il tempo

l'ombrello

la pioggia

il lampo

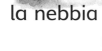
la nebbia

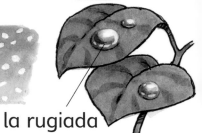
il sole

le
nuvo

il cielo

la neve

la rugiada

il vento

la foschita

la brina

l'arcobaleno

Le stagioni

la primavera

l'estate

l'autunno

l'inverno

Gli animali domestici

il criceto

il veterinario

la cuccia

il porcellino d'India

il cagnolino

il cane

il pappagallino

il pappagallo

il becco

il cibo

il coniglio

il canarino

la gabbia

il gatto

la cesta

il topolino

il gattino

il latte

i pesci rossi

Lo sport

il canottaggio

lo snowboard

la vela

il windsurf

la pallacanestro

la racchetta

il tennis

il football americano

la ginnastica artistica

il cricket

il karatè

la mazz

la palla

la pesca

la canna da pesca

l'esca

il rugby

la danza

il baseball

i tuffi

la piscina

il nuoto

la corsa campestre

il tiro con l'arco

il bersaglio

il volo libero

il jogging

il ciclismo

il casco

l'alpinismo

il judo

il calcio

il cavallo

il pony

l'armadietto

lo spogliatoio

l'equitazione

badminton

il ping-pong

i pattini

il pattinaggio su ghiaccio

i bastoncini da sci

la seggiovia

gli sci

lo sci

il sumo

51

I colori

l'arancione

il verde

il nero

il grigio

il ross

il marrone

il rosa

il viola

il giallo

il bianco

il blu

Le forme

il rettangolo

il cerchio

il rombo

il cono

la stella

il cubo

l'ovale

il triangolo

il quadrato

la falce di luna

numeri

uno

due

tre

quattro

cinque

sei

sette

otto

nove

dieci

undici

dodici

tredici

quattordici

quindici

sedici

diciassette

diciotto

diciannove

venti

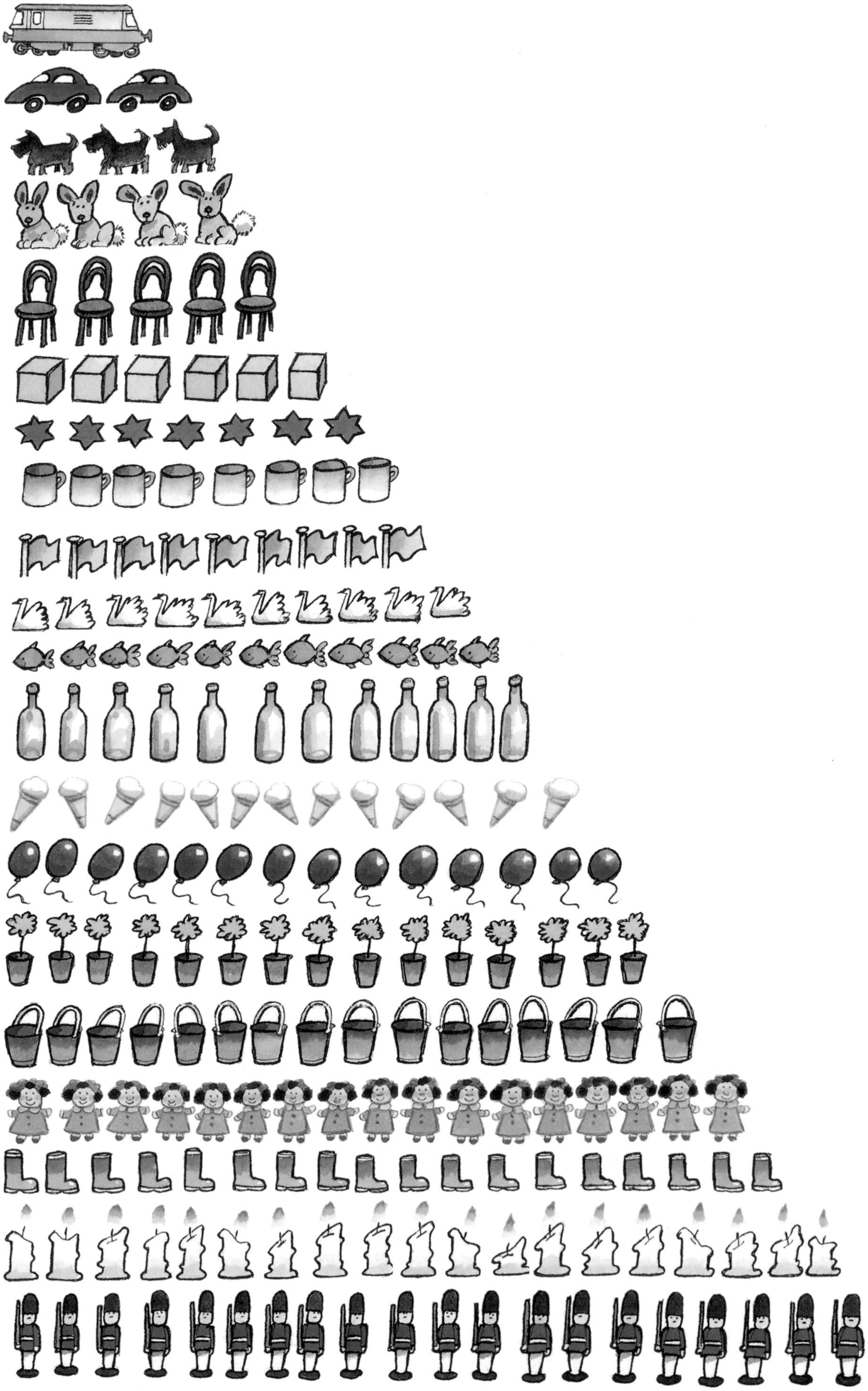

53

Il luna park

la ruota

la giostra

il tappetino

lo scivolo

il trenino dei fantasmi

il tiro al cerchietto

il pop-corn

le montagne russe

il tiro a segno

l'autoscontro

lo zucchero filato

54

Il circo

il funambolo

l'asta

il trapezio

camminare sulla corda

'equilibrista

la scala di corda

la rete di sicurezza

gli acrobati

il coniglio

il domatore

il cane

il cerchio

il cilindro

il giocoliere

il farfallino

l'orchestra

la cavallerizza

il pagliaccio

Word list

In this list, you can find all the Italian words in this book. They are listed in alphabetical order. Next to each one, you can see its pronunciation (how to say it) in letters *like this*, and then its English translation.

Remember that Italian nouns (words for things) are either masculine or feminine (see page 3). In the list, each one has **il**, **lo**, **la**, **l'**, **i**, **gli** or **le** in front of it. These all mean "the". The words with il or lo are masculine, those with la are feminine. Italian nouns that begin with "a", "e", "i", "o" or "u" have l' in front of them. After the word you will see (m) or (f) to show whether it is masculine or feminine.

Plural nouns (a noun is a plural if you are talking about more than one, for example "cats") have i or gli in front if they are masculine, or le if they are feminine.

About Italian pronunciation
Read the pronunciation as if it were an English word, but try to remember the following points about how Italian words are said:

All the letters in an Italian word are sounded, except 'h'; Dou letters, like 'll' or 'nn', sound a little longer than usual;

c before *e* or *i* is pronounced *ch*;
ch before *e* or *i* is pronounced *k*;
gh before *e* or *i* is pronounced *g* as in *get*;
sc before *e* or *i* is pronounced *sh*;
z is pronounced *ts*;

Most Italian words have a part that you stress, or say louder (like the "day" part of the English word "today"). So you kno which part of each word you should stress, it is shown in the letters ***like this*** in the pronunciation guide;

In the guide, *ay* is like the *a* in the date;

o is like the *o* in *hot*;
ow is like the *ow* in *cow*;
g is always like the *g* in *get*;
ly is like the *lli* in *million*;
ny is like the *ni* in *onion*;
ye is always like the *ye* in *yet*.

A

acchiappare	*akkyap**par**ay*	to catch
l'acqua (f)	***lak**wa*	water
gli acquarelli	*lyee akwa**rel**lee*	paints
l'acquario (m)	*lak**war**yo*	aquarium
gli acrobati	*lyee a**kro**batee*	acrobats
le addizioni	*lay addee**tsy**onee*	sums
l'aereo (m)	*la-**ay**rayo*	aeroplane
l'aeroporto	*la-ayro**por**to*	airport
gli agnelli	*lyee a**nyel**lee*	lambs
l'agricoltore	*lagreekol**tor**ay*	farmer
l'aiuola (f)	*la-**yu**ola*	flower bed
l'albergo (m)	***lal**bairgo*	hotel
gli alberi	*lyee **al**bairee*	trees
l'albero (m)	***lal**bairo*	tree
l'albero (m) di Natale	***lal**bairo dee na**ta**lay*	Christmas tree
l'albicocca (f)	*lalbee**kok**ka*	apricot
l'alfabeto (m)	*lalfa**bay**to*	alphabet
le alghe	*lay **al**gay*	seaweed
le ali	*lay **a**lee*	wings
l'alpinismo (m)	*lalpee**neez**mo*	climbing
l'altalena (f) a bilico	*lalta**lay**na a **bee**leeko*	seesaw
le altalene	*lay alta**lay**nay*	swings
alto	***al**to*	high
l'alveare (m)	*lalvay**ar**ay*	beehive
l'ambulanza (f)	*lamboo**lan**tsa*	ambulance
l'ananas (m)	***lan**anass*	pineapple
le anatre	*lay **an**atray*	ducks
gli anatroccoli	*lyee ana**trok**kolee*	ducklings
l'anello (m)	*la**nel**lo*	ring
gli animali domestici	*lyee a**nee**malee do**mes**teechee*	pets
l'annaffiatoio (m)	*lanaffya**to**yo*	watering can
l'annaffiatore (m)	*lanaffya**tor**ay*	sprinkler
l'antenna (f)	*lan**ten**na*	aerial
l'ape (f)	***la**pay*	bee
aperto	*a**pair**to*	open
l'aquila (f)	***lak**weela*	eagle
l'aquilone (m)	*lakwee**lo**nay*	kite
l'arancia (f)	*la**ran**cha*	orange (fruit)
l'arancione (m)	*aran**cho**nay*	orange (colour)
l'aratro (m)	*la**ra**tro*	plough
l'arco (m)	***lar**ko*	bow (and arrows)
l'arcobaleno (m)	*larkoba**lay**no*	rainbow
l'armadietto (m)	*larma**dye**tto*	cupboard
l'armadio (m)	*lar**ma**dyo*	wardrobe
l'armonica (f)	*lar**mo**neeka*	mouth organ
arrampicarsi	*arrampee**kar**see*	to climb
l'artista (m/f)	*lar**tee**sta*	artist
l'ascensore (m)	*lashen**sor**ay*	lift
l'ascia (f)	***la**sha*	axe
l'asciugamano (m)	*lashooga**ma**no*	towel
lo strofinaccio (m)	*eel strofee**na**cho*	tea towel
asciutto	*a**shoo**tto*	dry
ascoltare	*askol**tar**ay*	to listen
l'asino (m)	***la**zeeno*	donkey
le asole	*lay **a**zolay*	button holes
aspettare	*aspet**tar**ay*	to wait
l'aspirapolvere (m)	*laspeera**pol**vairay*	vacuum cleaner
l'asse (f)	***las**say*	plan
l'asse (f) da stiro	***las**say da **stee**ro*	board
l'asta (f)	***las**ta*	pole
l'astronave (f)	*lastro**na**vay*	spaceship
l'astronauta (m)	*lastro**now**ta*	astronaut
gli astronauti	*lyee astro**now**tee*	astronauts, spacemen
l'attaccapanni (m)	*lattakka**pan**nee*	pegs
l'attore (m)	*lat**tor**ay*	actor
l'attrice (f)	*lat**tree**chay*	actress
l'autobus (m)	***low**toboos*	bus
l'autocisterna (f)	*lowtochee**stair**na*	tanker lorry
l'autolavaggio (m)	*lowtola**vaj**jo*	car wash

utopompa (f)	lowto**pompa**	fire engine
utoscontro (m)	lowto**skontro**	dodgems
utunno (m)	low**toon**no	autumn
vvolgibile (m)	lavvol**jee**beelay	blind
azioni	lay a**tsy**onee	actions

abbo Natale	**bab**bo na**ta**lay	Father Christmas
bacchette	lay bak**ket**tay	chopsticks
budminton	eel **bad**meenton	badminton
agnato	ban**ya**to	wet
bagno	eel **ban**yo	bathroom
balena	la ba**lay**na	whale
allare	bal**la**ray	to dance
e balle di paglia	lay **bal**lay dee **pal**ya	straw bales
ballerini	ee ballai**ree**nee	dancers
bambina	la bam**bee**na	girl
bambini	ee bam**bee**nee	children
bambino	eel bam**bee**no	boy
e bambole	lay **bam**bolay	dolls
banana	la ba**na**na	banana
banco	eel **ban**ko	desk
bandiera	la ban**dyai**ra	flag
bar	eel bar	café
barattoli	ee ba**rat**tolee	pots, jars
barca	la **bar**ka	boat
barca a vela	la **bar**ka a **vay**la	sailing boat
barca a remi	la **bar**ka a **ray**mee	rowing boat
baseball	eel bayz**bol**	baseball
basso	**bas**so	low
bastone	eel ba**sto**nay	stick
bastoncini da sci	ee baston**chee**nee da shee	ski poles
la batteria	la battai**ree**a	battery
il bebè	eel be**bay**	baby
il becco	eel **bek**ko	beak
la benzina	la ben**tsee**na	petrol
bere	**bai**ray	to drink
il berretto	eel bair**ret**to	cap
il bersaglio	eel bair**sal**yo	target
il bianco	eel **byan**ko	white
i bicchieri	ee beek**kyai**ree	glasses (for drinking)
la bicicletta	la beechee**klet**ta	bicycle
le biglie	lay **beel**yay	marbles
la biglietteria automatica	la beelyettai**ree**a owto**ma**teeka	ticket machine
il biglietto di auguri	eel beel**yet**to dee ow**goo**ree	birthday card
la bilancia	la bee**lan**cha	scales
i binari	ee bee**na**ree	railway track
il biscotto	eel bee**skot**to	biscuit
il bisonte	eel bee**zon**tay	bison
il blu	eel bloo	blue
la bocca	la **bok**ka	mouth
il bollitore	eel bollee**to**ray	kettle
la borsa	la **bor**sa	handbag
la borsa della spesa	la **bor**sa **del**la **spay**za	carrier bag
il borsellino	eel borsel**lee**no	wallet
la botte	la **bot**tay	barrel
le bottiglie	lay bot**teel**yay	bottles
i bottoni	ee bot**to**nee	buttons
il braccio	eel **bra**cho	arm
la brina	la **bree**na	frost
il bruco	eel **broo**ko	caterpillar
la buca di sabbia	la **boo**ka dee **sab**bya	sandpit
il buco	eel **boo**ko	hole
le bullette	lay **bool**letay	tacks

i bulloni	ee bool**lo**nee	bolts
buono	**bwo**no	good
il burro	eel **boor**ro	butter

C

il cacciavite	eel kacha**vee**tay	screwdriver
cadere	ka**dai**ray	to fall
il caffè	eel kaf**fay**	coffee
il cagnolino	eel kanyo**lee**no	puppy
il calcio	eel **kal**cho	football
caldo	**kal**do	hot
il calendario	eel kalen**dar**yo	calendar
la calzamaglia	la kaltsa**mal**ya	tights
i calzini	ee kal**tsee**nee	socks
la camera da letto	la **ka**maira da **let**to	bedroom
la cameriera	la kamai**ryai**ra	waitress
il cameriere	eel kamai**ryai**ray	waiter
la camicia	la ka**mee**cha	shirt
la camicia da notte	la ka**mee**cha da **not**tay	nightdress
il camion	eel **ka**myon	lorry
il/la camionista	la kamyo**nee**sta	lorry driver
camminare	kammee**na**ray	to walk
camminare a carponi	kammee**na**ray a kar**po**nee	to crawl
camminare sulla corda	kammee**na**ray **sool**la **kor**da	to walk a tightrope
la campagna	la kam**pan**ya	country
il campo	eel **kam**po	field
il campo giochi	eel **kam**po **jo**kee	playground
il canale	eel ka**na**lay	canal
il canarino	eel kana**ree**no	canary
la cancellata	la kanchel**la**ta	railings
il cancello	eel kan**chel**lo	gate
la candela	la kan**day**la	candle
le candeline	lay kande**lee**nay	cake candles
il cane	eel **ka**nay	dog
il cane pastore	eel **ka**nay pa**sto**ray	sheepdog
il canguro	eel kan**goo**ro	kangaroo
la canna da pesca	la **kan**na da **pes**ka	fishing rod
la cannuccia	la kan**noo**cha	straw
la canoa	la ka**no**a	canoe
il canottaggio	eel kanot**taj**jo	rowing
la canottiera	la kanot**tyai**ra	vest
i cantanti	ee kan**tan**tee	singers
cantare	kan**ta**ray	to sing
il capannone	eel kapan**no**nay	barn
i capelli	ee ka**pel**lee	hair
il cappello	eel kap**pel**lo	hat
il cappello da sole	eel kap**pel**lo da **so**lay	sun hat
il cappotto	eel kap**pot**to	coat
la capra	la **ka**pra	goat
la caramella	la kara**mel**la	sweet
il cardigan	eel **kar**deegan	cardigan
la carne	la **kar**nay	meat
la carota	la ka**ro**ta	carrot
il carrello	eel kar**rel**lo	trolley
il carretto	eel kar**ret**to	cart
la carriola	la kar**ryo**la	wheelbarrow
il carro attrezzi	eel **kar**ro at**tret**tsee	breakdown lorry
la carrozzina	la karrot**tsee**na	pram
la carta	la **kar**ta	paper
la carta geografica	la **kar**ta jayo**gra**feeka	map
la carta igienica	la **kar**ta ee**jen**eeka	toilet paper
la carta vetrata	la **kar**ta ve**tra**ta	sandpaper
il cartello stradale	eel kar**tel**lo stra**da**lay	signpost

le cartoline	lay kartoleenay	cards
la casa	la kaza	house
la casa colonica	la kaza koloneeka	farmhouse
la casa delle bambole	la kaza dellay bambolay	dolls' house
la cascata	la kaskata	waterfall
il casco	eel kasko	helmet
il casotto	eel kazotto	shed
la cassa	la kassa	checkout
la cassetta degli arnesi	la kassetta delyee arnaysee	tool box
il cassetto	eel kassetto	drawer
il cassettone	eel kassettonay	chest of drawers
il castello	eel kastello	castle
il castello di sabbia	eel kastello dee sabbya	sandcastle
il castoro	eel kastoro	beaver
cattivo	katteevo	bad
la cavallerizza	la kavallaireettsa	bareback rider
il cavalletto	eel kavalletto	easel
il cavallo	eel kavallo	horse
il cavallo a dondolo	eel kavallo a dondolo	rocking horse
il cavolfiore	eel kavolfyoray	cauliflower
il cavolo	eel kavolo	cabbage
la cena	la chayna	supper, dinner
i ceppi	ee cheppee	logs
il cerchio	eel chairkyo	circle, hoop
i cereali	ee chairayalee	cereal
la cerniera lampo	la chairnyaira lampo	zip
il cerotto	eel chairotto	sticking plaster
il cervo	eel chairvo	deer
il cespuglio	eel chespoolyo	bush
la cesta	la chesta	basket
il cestino	eel chesteeno	shopping basket
il cestino della carta	eel chesteeno della karta	waste paper basket
il cetriolo	eel chetreeolo	cucumber
chiaro	kyaro	light
la chiatta	la kyatta	barge
la chiave	la kyavay	key
la chiave inglese	la kyavay eenglayzay	spanner
la chiocciola	la kyochola	snail
i chiodi	ee kyodee	nails
la chitarra	la keetarra	guitar
la chiusa	la kyooza	lock (canal)
chiuso	kyoozo	closed
il cibo in scatola	eel cheebo een skatola	tinned food
il cibo	eel cheebo	food
il ciclismo	eel cheekleezmo	cycling
il cielo	eel chaylo	sky
i cigni	ee cheenyee	swans
la ciliegia	la cheelyeja	cherry
il cilindro	eel cheeleendro	cylinder
il cinema	eel cheenayma	cinema
cinque	cheenquay	five
la cintura	la cheentoora	belt
la cioccolata	la chokkolata	chocolate
la cioccolata calda	la chokkolata kalda	hot chocolate
i ciottoli	ee chottolee	pebbles
la cipolla	la cheepolla	onion
il circo	eel cheerko	circus
la coccinella	la kocheenella	ladybird
il coccodrillo	eel kokkodreello	crocodile
la coda	la koda	tail
il cofano	eel kofano	bonnet
la colazione	la kolatsyonay	breakfast
la colla	la kola	glue
la collana	la kollana	necklace
la collina	la kolleena	hill
il collo	eel kollo	neck
i colori	ee koloree	colours, paints
i colori per il viso	ee koloree pair eel veezo	face paints
i coltelli	ee koltellee	knives
il comignolo	eel komeenyolo	chimney
il Compact Disc	eel kompat deesk	CD
il compleanno	eel komplayanno	birthday
comprare	kompraray	to buy
il computer	eel kompyootair	computer
la conchiglia	la konkeelya	shell
il conducente di autobus	eel kondoochentay dee owtoboos	bus driver
le condutture	lay kondoottooray	pipes
il coniglio	eel koneelyo	rabbit
il cono	eel kono	cone
i contrari	ee kontraree	opposites
il controllore	eel kontrolloray	ticket inspector
la corda per saltare	la korda pair saltaray	skipping rope
le corna	lay korna	horns
correre	korrairay	to run
la corsa campestre	la korsa kampestray	running race
corto	korto	short
le costruzioni	lay kostrootsyonee	building blocks
il costume da bagno	eel kostoomay da banyo	swimsuit
i costumi	ee kostoomee	fancy dress
il cotone idrofilo	eel kotonay eedrofeelo	cotton wool
la cravatta	la kravatta	tie
il criceto	eel kreechayto	hamster
il cricket	eel kreeket	cricket
il cubo	eel koobo	cube
i cucchiaini	ee kookkya-eenee	teaspoons
la cuccia	la koocha	kennel
la cucina	la koocheena	kitchen
cucinare	koocheenaray	to cook
cucire	koocheeray	to sew
il cugino	eel koojeeno	cousin
il cuoco	eel kwoko	cook
il cuscino	eel koosheeno	cushion

D

i dadi (da officina)	ee dadee (da offeecheena)	nuts (workshop)
i dadi (per giocare)	ee dadee (pair jokaray)	dice
la damigella d'onore	la dameejella donoray	bridesmaid
la danza	la dantsa	dancing
davanti	davantee	front
le decorazioni di carta	lay dekoratsyonee dee karta	paper chains
il delfino	eel delfeeno	dolphin
i denti	ee dentee	teeth
il dentifricio	eel denteefreecho	toothpaste
il/la dentista	eel/la denteesta	dentist
dentro	dentro	inside
destra	destra	right
il detersivo	eel detairseevo	washing powder
diciannove	deechannovay	nineteen
diciassette	deechassettay	seventeen
diciotto	deechotto	eighteen
dieci	dyechee	ten
dietro	dyetro	behind
difficile	deeffeecheelay	difficult
dipingere	deepeenjairay	to paint
il disegno	eel deesenyo	drawing

distributore di benzina	eel eestreeboo**tor**ay dee ben**tsee**na	petrol pump
e dita dei piedi	lay **dee**ta day **pye**dee	toes
e dita della mano	lay **dee**ta **del**la **ma**no	fingers
l divano	eel **dee**vano	sofa
a doccia	la **do**cha	shower
dodici	**do**deechee	twelve
dolci	ee **dol**chee	pudding
l domatore	eel doma**tor**ay	ringmaster
domenica	dome**nee**ka	Sunday
la donna	la **don**na	woman
dormire	dor**meer**ay	to sleep
il dottore	eel dot**tor**ay	doctor
la dottoressa	la dotto**res**sa	(woman) doctor
il dromedario	eel drome**dar**y	camel
due	**doo**ay	two
duro	**doo**ro	hard

E

l'elefante (m)	lele**fan**tay	elephant
l'elicottero (m)	lelee**kot**tairo	helicopter
l'equilibrista (m)	lekweelee**brees**ta	tightrope walker
l'equitazione (f)	lekweeta**tsy**onay	riding
l'erba (f)	**lair**ba	grass
l'esca (f)	**les**ka	bait
l'estate (f)	le**sta**tay	summer

F

la fabbrica	la **fab**breeka	factory
facile	**fa**cheelay	easy
i fagiolini	ee fajo**lee**nee	beans
la falce di luna	la **fal**chay dee **loo**na	crescent
il falegname	eel fale**nya**may	carpenter
la falena	la fa**lay**na	moth
il falò	eel fa**lo**	bonfire
la famiglia	la fa**meel**ya	family
il fango	eel **fan**go	mud
fare	**far**ay	to make, to do
fare a botte	**far**ay a **bot**tay	to fight
la farfalla	la far**fal**la	butterfly
il farfallino	eel farfal**lee**no	bow tie
la farina	la fa**ree**na	flour
il faro	eel **far**o	lighthouse
la fascia	la **fa**sha	bandage
la fattoria	la fatto**ree**a	farm
i fazzoletti di carta	ee fattso**let**tee dee **kar**ta	tissues
il fazzoletto	eel fattso**let**to	handkerchief
la felpa	la **fel**pa	sweatshirt
il ferro da stiro	eel **fair**ro da **steer**o	iron
la festa	la **fes**ta	party
i fiammiferi	ee fyam**mee**fairee	matches
la fibbia	la **feeb**bya	buckle
il fienile	eel fye**nee**lay	hay loft
il fieno	eel **fye**no	hay
la figlia	la **feel**ya	daughter
il figlio	eel **feel**yo	son
la finestra	la fee**nes**tra	window
i fiori	ee **fyor**ee	flowers
il fischietto	eel fees**kyet**to	whistle
il fiume	eel **fyoo**may	river
il flauto dolce	eel **flow**to **dol**chay	recorder
la foca	la **fo**ka	seal
le foglie	lay **fol**yay	leaves

il football americano	eel **foot**bol amaire**ka**no	American football
le forbici	lay **for**beechee	scissors
le forchette	lay for**ket**tay	forks
il forcone	eel for**ko**nay	garden fork
la foresta	la fo**res**ta	forest
il formaggio	eel for**maj**jo	cheese
le forme	lay **for**may	shapes
il fornaio	eel for**na**-yo	baker (man)
la fornaia	la for**na**-ya	baker (woman)
la foschia	la **fos**kya	mist
le fotografie	lay fotogra**fee**-ay	photos
il fotografo	eel fo**to**grafo	photographer
la fragola	la **fra**gola	strawberry
il fratello	eel fra**tel**lo	brother
le frecce	lay **fre**chay	arrows
freddo	**fred**do	cold
il frigorifero	eel freego**ree**fairo	fridge
la frittata	la freet**ta**ta	omelette
le frittelle	lay freet**tel**lay	pancakes
la frutta	la **froot**ta	fruit
il frutteto	eel frut**tay**to	orchard
il fucile	eel foo**chee**lay	gun
il fumetto	eel foo**met**to	comic
il fumo	eel **foo**mo	smoke
il funambolo	eel foo**nam**bolo	tightrope walker
la fune	la **foo**nay	rope
il fungo	eel **foon**go	mushroom
i fuochi d'artificio	ee **fwo**kee dartee**fee**cho	fireworks
fuori	**fwor**ee	outside
il furgone	eel foor**go**nay	van

G

la gabbia	la **gab**bya	cage
il gabbiano	eel gab**by**ano	seagull
la galleria	la gallai**ree**a	tunnel
le galline	lay gal**lee**nay	hens
il gallo	eel **gal**lo	cockerel
la gamba	la **gam**ba	leg
il gattino	eel gat**tee**no	kitten
il gatto	eel **gat**to	cat
il gelato	eel je**la**to	ice cream
i gessetti	ee jes**set**tee	chalks
il gesso	eel **jes**so	plaster
il giallo	eel **jal**lo	yellow
il giardino	eel jar**dee**no	garden
la ginnastica artistica	la jeen**nas**teeka ar**tees**teeka	gymnastics
il ginocchio	eel jee**nok**kyo	knee
giocare	jo**kar**ay	to play
i giocattoli	ee jo**kat**tolee	toys
il giocoliere	eel joko**lyair**ay	juggler
il giornale	eel jor**na**lay	newspaper
i giorni	ee **jor**nee	days
i giorni speciali	ee **jor**nee spe**cha**lee	special days
la giostra	la **jos**tra	merry-go-round
giovedì	jove**dee**	Thursday
la giraffa	la jee**raf**fa	giraffe
i girini	ee jee**ree**nee	tadpoles
giù	**joo**	down
il giubbotto	eel joob**bot**to	waistcoat
il giudice	eel **joo**deecha	judge
il gomito	eel **go**meeto	elbow
la gomma	la **gom**ma	rubber
la gonna	la **gon**na	skirt
il gorilla	eel go**reel**la	gorilla

il granchio	eel **gran**kyo	crab
grande	**gran**day	big
grasso	**gras**so	fat
il grembiule	eel grem**byoo**lay	apron
il grigio	eel **gree**jo	grey
la gru	la groo	crane
le grucce	lay **groo**chay	crutches
la guancia	la **gwan**cha	cheek
il guanciale	eel gwan**cha**lay	pillow
i guanti	ee **gwan**tee	gloves
guardare	gwar**dar**ay	to look
il guinzaglio	eel gween**tsa**lyo	lead
il gufo	eel **goo**fo	owl

H

l'hamburger (m)	**lam**boorgair	hamburger
l'hostess (f)	**los**tess	air hostess

I

l'iceberg (m)	**lies**bairg	iceberg
l'imbianchino (m)	leembyan**kee**no	house painter
in cima	een **chee**ma	on top
in fondo	een **fon**do	at the bottom
l'infermiere (m)	leenfair**myair**ay	nurse (man)
l'infermiera (f)	leenfair**myair**a	nurse (woman)
l'ingresso (m)	een**gres**so	hall
l'insalata (f)	leensa**la**ta	salad
l'insegnante (m/f)	leense**nyan**tay	teacher
l'interruttore (m)	leentairroot**tor**ay	switch
l'inverno (m)	leen**vair**no	winter
l'ippopotamo (m)	leeppo**po**tamo	hippopotamus
l'isola (f)	**lee**zola	island

J

i jeans	ee jeens	jeans
il jogging	eel **jog**geeng	jogging
il judo	eel **joo**do	judo

K

il karatè	eel kara**tay**	karate
il ketchup	eel **ke**chap	ketchup

L

le labbra	lay **lab**bra	lips
il laboratorio	eel labora**tor**yo	workshop
i lacci per le scarpe	ee **la**chee pair lay **skar**pay	shoelaces
il lago	eel **la**go	luke
la lampada	la **lam**pada	lamp
la lampadina	la lampa**dee**na	light bulb
il lampione	eel lam**pyo**nay	street lamp
il lampo	eel **lam**po	lightning
il lampone	eel lam**po**nay	raspberry
lanciare	lan**char**ay	to throw

il latte	eel **lat**tay	milk
la lattuga	la lat**too**ga	lettuce
la lavagna	la la**van**ya	board
il lavandino	eel lavan**dee**no	basin
lavarsi	la**var**see	to wash
la lavatrice	la lava**tree**chay	washing machine
il lavello	eel la**vel**lo	sink
lavorare a maglia	lavo**rar**ay a **mal**ya	to knit
leggere	**lej**jairay	to read
il legno	eel **len**yo	wood
lento	**len**to	slow
il lenzuolo	eel len**tswo**lo	sheet
i leoncini	ee layon**chee**ne	lion cubs
il leone	eel la**yo**nay	lion
il leopardo	eel layo**par**do	leopard
le lettere	lay **let**tairay	letters
il letto	eel **let**to	bed
i libri	ee **lee**bree	books
la lima	la **lee**ma	file
il limone	eel lee**mo**nay	lemon
la lingua	la **leen**gwa	tongue
il locomotore	eel lokomo**tor**ay	engine (train)
lontano	lon**ta**no	far
la lucertola	la loo**chair**tola	lizard
la luna	la **loo**na	moon
il luna park	eel **loo**na park	funfair
lunedì	Loonay**dee**	Monday
lungo	**Loon**go	long
il lupo	eel **loo**po	wolf

M

la macchina	la **ma**keena	car
la macchina da corsa	la **ma**keena da **kor**sa	racing car
la macchina della polizia	la **ma**keena **del**la polee**tsee**a	police car
la macchina fotografica	la **ma**kkeena foto**gra**feeka	camera
il macchinista	eel makkee**nees**ta	train driver
il macellaio	eel machel**la**-yo	butcher
la madre	la **ma**dray	mother
la maglietta	la mal**yet**ta	tee-shirt
il maglione	eel mal**yo**nay	pull-over
magro	**ma**gro	thin
i maiali	ee ma-**ya**lee	pigs
i maialini	ee ma-ya**lee**nee	piglets
il mandarino	eel manda**ree**no	clementine
mangiare	man**jar**ay	to eat
la maniglia della porta	la ma**neel**ya **del**la **por**ta	door handle
la mano	la **ma**no	hand
il mappamondo	eel mappa**mon**do	globe
il marciapiede	eel marcha**pye**day	pavement
il mare	eel **ma**ray	sea
il marinaio	eel maree**na**-yo	sailor
le marionette	lay maryo**net**tay	puppets
il marito	eel ma**ree**to	husband
la marmellata	la marmel**la**ta	jam
il marrone	eel mar**ro**nay	brown
martedì	marte**dee**	Tuesday
il martello	eel mar**tel**lo	hammer
il martello pneumatico	eel mar**tel**lo pnayooma**tee**ko	pneumatic drill
le maschere	lay **mas**kairay	masks
i massi	ee **mas**see	rocks
la matita	la ma**tee**ta	pencil

il matrimonio	eel matreemonyo	wedding
la mattina	la matteena	morning
le mattonelle	lay mattonellay	tiles
i mattoni	ee mattonee	bricks
la mazza	la mattsa	bat (sports)
me stesso	may stesso	myself
i meccanici	ee mekkaneechee	mechanics
la medicina	la medeecheena	medicine
la mela	la mayla	apple
il melone	eel maylonay	melon
il mento	eel mento	chin
il mercato	eel mairkato	market
mercoledì	mairkolaydee	Wednesday
i mestieri	ee mestyairee	jobs
i mestoli	ee mestolee	wooden spoons
il metro	eel metro	tape measure
il miele	eel myelay	honey
la minestra	la meenestra	soup
la moglie	la molyay	wife
molti	moltee	many
la mongolfiera	la mongolfyaira	hot air balloon
la montagna	la montanya	mountain
le montagne russe	lay montanyay roossay	rollercoaster
la moquette	la mokett	fitted carpet
morbido	morbeedo	soft
la morsa	la morsa	vice
morto	morto	dead
la mosca	la moska	fly
la motocicletta	la motocheekletta	motorbike
il motore	eel motoray	engine (car)
il motoscafo	eel motoskafo	motor boat
la mucca	la mookka	cow
il mucchio di fieno	eel mookkyo dee fyeno	haystack
il mulino a vento	eel mooleeno a vento	windmill
la musicassetta	la moozeekassetta	cassette
le mutande	lay mootanday	underpants

N

nascondersi	naskondairsee	to hide
il naso	eel nazo	nose
il nastro	eel nastro	ribbon
Natale	natalay	Christmas
la nave	la navay	ship
la nebbia	la nebbya	fog
il negozio	eel negotsyo	shop
il nero	eel nairo	black
la neve	la nayvay	snow
il nido	eel needo	nest
la nonna	la nonna	grandmother
il nonno	eel nonno	grandfather
la notte	la nottay	night
nove	novay	nine
i numeri	ee noomairee	numbers
il nuoto	eel nwoto	swimming
nuovo	nwovo	new
le nuvole	lay noovolay	clouds

O

l'occhio (m)	lokkyo	eye
le oche	lay okay	geese
l'olio (m)	lolyo	oil
l'ombrello (m)	lombrello	umbrella
l'ombrellone (m)	lombrellonay	beach umbrella
le onde	lay onday	waves
l'orchestra (f)	lorkestra	orchestra
le orecchie	lay orekkyay	ears
l'orologio (m)	lorolojo	clock, watch
l'orsacchiotto (m)	lorsakkyotto	teddy bear
l'orso (m)	lorso	bear
l'orso (m) polare	lorso polaray	polar bear
l'ospedale (m)	lospedalay	hospital
l'osso (m)	losso	bone
otto	otto	eight
l'ovale (m)	lovalay	oval

P

la padella	la padella	frying pan
il padre	eel padray	father
la pagaia	la paga-ya	paddle
il pagliaccio	eel palyacho	clown
il palazzo	eel palattso	block of flats, building
la paletta (da giardino)	la paletta (da jardeeno)	trowel
la paletta (da spiaggia)	la paletta (da spyajja)	beach spade
la paletta (per la pazzatura)	la paletta (pair la pattsatoora)	dustpan
la palla	la palla	ball
la pallacanestro	la pallakanestro	basketball
il palloncino	eel palloncheeno	balloon
la panchina	la pankeena	bench
la pancia	la pancha	tummy
il panda	eel panda	panda
il pane	eel panay	bread
il pane tostato	eel panay tostato	toast
il panino	eel paneeno	sandwich
la panna	la panna	cream
il pannolino	eel pannoleeno	nappy
i pantaloncini	ee pantaloncheenee	shorts
i pantaloni	ee pantalonee	trousers
le pantofole	lay pantofolay	slippers
il pappagallino	eel pappagalleeno	budgerigar
il pappagallo	eel pappagallo	parrot
il paracadute	eel parakadootay	parachute
il parco	eel parko	park
la parete	la paraytay	wall
parlare	parlaray	to talk
il parrucchiere	eel parrookkyairay	hairdresser
il passeggino	eel passejjeeno	pushchair
i pastelli	ee pastellee	crayons
i pasti	ee pastee	meals
la pastorella	la pastorella	shepherdess
le patate	lay patatay	potatoes
le patatine	lay patateenay	crisps
le patatine fritte	lay patateenay freettay	chips
il pattinaggio su ghiaccio	eel patteenajjio soo gyacho	ice skating
i pattini	ee patteenee	skates
la pattumiera	la pattoomyaira	rubbish bin
il pavimento	eel paveemento	floor
le pecore	lay paykoray	sheep
il pellicano	eel pelleekano	pelican
la penna	la penna	pen
i pennarelli	ee pennarellee	felt-tips
il pennello	eel pennello	paintbrush

pensare	pensaray	to think
la pensilina	la penseeleena	platform
le pentole	le pentolay	pans
il pepe	eel paypay	pepper
la pera	a paira	pear
le perline	lay pairleenay	beads
la pesca (frutto)	la peska (frootto)	peach
la pesca (attività)	la peska (atteeveeta)	fishing
il pescatore	eel peskatoray	fisherman
il pesce	eel peshay	fish
il peschereccio	eel peskairecho	fishing boat
i pesci rossi	ee peshee rossee	goldfish
la petroliera	la petrolyaira	oil tanker
il pettine	eel petteenay	comb
la pialla	la pyalla	plane (shaving)
il pianeta	eel pyanayta	planet
piangere	pyanjairay	to cry
il piano di lavoro	eel pyano dee lavoro	workbench
il pianoforte	eel pyanofortay	piano
la pianta	la pyanta	plant
i piatti	ee pyattee	plates
i piattini	ee pyatteenee	saucers
il piccione	eel peechonay	pigeon
piccolo	peekkolo	small
il picnic	eel peekneek	picnic
il piede	eel pyeday	foot
pieno	pyeno	full
le pietre	lay pyetray	stones
il pigiama	eel peejama	pyjamas
le pillole	lay peellolay	pills
il pilota	eel peelota	pilot
il ping-pong	eel peeng-pong	ping-pong
il pinguino	eel peengweeno	penguin
le pinne	lay peennay	flippers
la pioggia	la pyojja	rain
il pipistrello	eel peepeestrello	bat (animal)
la piscina	la peesheena	swimming pool
i piselli	ee peezellee	peas
la pista di atterraggio	la peesta dee attairrajjo	runway
le piume	lay pyoomay	feathers
il piumone	eel pyoomonay	duvet
la pizza	la peettsa	pizza
la plastilina	la plasteeleena	modelling dough
lo pneumatico	lo pnayoomateeko	tyre
pochi	pokee	few
i poliziotti	ee poleetsyottee	policemen
il pollaio	eel polla-yo	hen-house
il pollice	eel polleechay	thumb
il pollo	eel pollo	chicken
il pomodoro	eel pomodoro	tomato
il pompelmo	eel pompelmo	grapefruit
il pompiere	eel pompyairay	fireman
il ponte	eel pontay	bridge
il pony	eel ponee	pony
il pop-corn	eel pop-korn	popcorn
il porcellino d'India	eel porchelleeno deendya	guinea pig
il porcile	eel porcheelay	pigsty
il porro	eel porro	leek
la porta	la porta	door
il portabagagli	eel portabagalyee	boot (of car)
portare	portaray	to carry
i poster	ee postair	posters
il postino	eel posteeno	postman
la pozzanghera	la pottsangaira	puddle
il pranzo	eel prantso	lunch, dinner
prendere	prendairay	to take
la primavera	la preemavaira	spring

primo	preemo	first
la proboscide	la probosheeday	trunk
il prosciutto	eel proshootto	ham
i pulcini	ee poolcheenee	chickens
pulito	pooleeto	clean
le puntine da disegno	lay poonteenay da deesenyo	drawing pins
il purè	eel pooray	mashed potato
il puzzle	eel pazol	puzzle

Q

il quaderno	eel kwadairno	notebook
il quadrato	eel kwadrato	square
quattordici	kwattordeechee	fourteen
quattro	kwattro	four
quindici	kweendeechee	fifteen

R

la racchetta	la rakketta	racquet
raccogliere	rakkolyairay	to pick
il radiatore	eel radyatoray	radiator
la radio	la radyo	radio
la ragnatela	la ranyatayla	spider's web
il ragno	eel ranyo	spider
i ramoscelli	ee ramoshellee	twigs
la rana	la rana	frog
il rastrello	eel rastrello	rake
il razzo	eel rattso	rocket
il regalo	eel regalo	present
il remo	eel remo	oar
la renna	la renna	reindeer
i respingenti	ee respeenjentee	buffers
la rete	la raytay	net
la rete di sicurezza	la raytay dee seekoorettsa	safety net
il rettangolo	eel rettangolo	rectangle
il riccio	eel reecho	hedgehog
ridere	reedairay	to laugh
il righello	eel reegello	ruler
il rimorchio	eel reemorkyo	trailer
il rinoceronte	eel reenochairontay	rhinoceros
il riso	eel reezo	rice
il robot	eel robot	robot
i rollerblades	ee rollerblades	rollerblades
il rombo	eel rombo	diamond (shape)
rompere	rompairay	to break
il rosa	eel roza	pink
il rospo	eel rospo	toad
il rosso	eel rosso	red
la roulotte	la roolott	caravan
il rubinetto	eel roobeenetto	tap
il rugby	eel ragbee	rugby
la rugiada	la roojada	dew
la ruota	la rwota	wheel, big wheel
il ruscello	eel rooshello	stream

S

sabato	sabato	Saturday
la sala d'aspetto	la sala daspetto	waiting room
il salame	eel salamay	salami
il sale	eel salay	salt

la salsiccia	la sal**see**cha	sausage
saltare	sal**tar**ay	to jump
saltare la corda	sal**tar**ay la **kor**da	to skip
il salvadanaio	eel salvada**na**-yo	money box
i sandali	ee **san**dalee	sandals
il sapone	eel sa**po**nay	soap
la scala	la **ska**la	ladder
la scala di corda	la **ska**la dee **kor**da	rope ladder
le scale	lay **ska**lay	stairs
gli scalini	lyee ska**lee**nee	steps
le scarpe	lay **skar**pay	shoes
le scarpe da ginnastica	lay **skar**pay da jeen**nas**teeka	trainers
la scatola	la **ska**tola	box
scavare	ska**var**ay	to dig
la scavatrice	la skava**tree**chay	bulldozer
lo schiacciasassi	lo skyacha**sas**see	roller
la schiena	la **skye**na	back
gli sci	lyee shee	skis
lo sci	lo shee	skiing
lo sci nautico	lo shee **now**teeko	waterskiing
la sciarpa	la **shar**pa	scarf
la scimmia	la **sheem**mya	monkey
lo scivolo	lo **shee**volo	slide, helter-skelter
le scodelle	lay sko**del**lay	bowls
la scogliera	la sko**lyai**ra	cliff
lo scoiattolo	lo sko**yat**tolo	squirrel
la scopa	la **sko**pa	broom
scrivere	**skree**vairay	to write
la scuderia	la skoodai**ree**a	stable
la scuola	la **skwo**la	school
scuro	**skoo**ro	dark
il secchiello	eel sek**kyel**lo	bucket
il sedano	eel **se**dano	celery
il sedere	eel se**dair**ay	bottom
la sedia	la **se**dya	chair
la sedia a rotelle	la **se**dya a ro**tel**lay	wheelchair
la sedia a sdraio	la **se**dya a **zdra**-yo	deckchair
sedici	**say**deechee	sixteen
la sega	la **say**ga	saw
la segatura	la sayga**too**ra	sawdust
la seggiovia	la sejjo**vee**a	chairlift
i segnali	ee sen**ya**lee	signals
sei	say	six
la sella	la **sel**la	saddle
il semaforo	eel se**ma**foro	traffic lights
i semi	ee **say**mee	seeds
il sentiero	eel sen**tya**iro	path
la sera	la **sai**ra	evening
il serpente	eel sair**pen**tay	snake
la serra	la **sair**ra	greenhouse
sette	**set**tay	seven
lo sgabello	lo zga**bel**lo	stool
la siepe	la **sye**pay	hedge
sinistra	see**nee**stra	left
la siringa	la see**reen**ga	syringe
lo skateboard	lo **sket**bord	skateboard
la slitta	la **sleet**ta	sleigh
lo snowboard	lo **sno**bord	snowboard
soffiare	sof**fya**ray	to blow
il soffitto	eel sof**feet**to	ceiling
il soggiorno	eel soj**jor**no	living room
i soldatini	ee solda**tee**nee	toy soldiers
i soldi	ee **sol**dee	money
il sole	eel **so**lay	sun
sopra	**so**pra	above
le sopracciglia	lay sopra**chee**lya	eyebrows
la sorella	la so**rel**la	sister
sorridere	sor**ree**dairay	to smile
sotto	**sot**to	below
il sottomarino	eel sotto**ma**reeno	submarine
spaccare	spak**kar**ay	to chop
gli spaghetti	lyee spa**get**tee	spaghetti
lo spago	lo **spa**go	string
le spalle	lay **spal**lay	shoulders
lo spaventapasseri	lo spaventa**pas**sairee	scarecrow
lo Spazio	lo **spat**syo	space
spazzare	spat**tsar**ay	to sweep
la spazzatura	la spattsa**too**ra	rubbish
la spazzola	la **spat**tsola	brush, hairbrush
lo spazzolino	lo spattso**lee**no	toothbrush
lo spazzolone	lo spattso**lo**nay	mop
lo specchio	lo **spek**kyo	mirror
la spiaggia	la **spya**jja	beach
la spilla	la **speel**la	badge
gli spinaci	lyee spee**na**chee	spinach
spingere	**speen**jairay	to push
lo spogliatoio	lo spolya**to**yo	changing room
sporco	**spor**ko	dirty
lo sport	lo sport	sport
la sposa	la **spo**za	bride
lo sposo	lo **spo**zo	bridegroom
la spugna	la **spoon**ya	sponge
lo squalo	lo **skwa**lo	shark
la staccionata	la stacho**na**ta	fence
le stagioni	lay sta**jo**nee	seasons
lo stagno	lo **stan**yo	pond
la stalla	la **stal**la	cowshed
stare seduti	**star**ay se**doo**tee	to sit
la stazione di servizio	la stat**syo**nay dee sair**veet**syo	garage
la stazione ferroviaria	la stat**syo**nay fairro**vyar**ya	station
la stella	la **stel**la	star
la stella marina	la **stel**la ma**ree**na	starfish
lo steward	lo **styoo**ward	air steward
gli stivali di gomma	lyee stee**va**lee dee **gom**ma	boots, wellies
lo straccio	lo **stra**cho	duster
la strada	la **stra**da	street
le strisce pedonali	lay **stree**shay pedo**na**lee	pedestrian crossing
lo struzzo	lo **stroot**tso	ostrich
su	soo	up
il subacqueo	eel soo**bak**kwayo	diver
il succo di frutta	eel **sook**ko dee **froot**ta	fruit juice
il sumo	eel **soo**mo	sumo wrestling
la susina	la soo**zee**na	plum

T

i tacchini	ee tak**kee**nee	turkeys
tagliare	ta**lyar**ay	to cut
la talpa	la **tal**pa	mole
i tamburi	ee tam**boo**ree	drums
il tappetino	eel tappay**tee**no	rug
il tappeto	eel tap**pay**to	carpet
la tartaruga	la tarta**roo**ya	tortoise
le tasche	lay **tas**kay	pockets
il tasso	eel **tas**so	badger
il tavolino	eel tavo**lee**no	small table
il taxi	eel **tak**see	taxi
le tazze	lay **tat**tsay	cups
il tè	eel tay	tea
la teiera	la ta**yai**ra	teapot

il telefono	*eel te**le**fono*	telephone
il telescopio	*eel tele**sko**pyo*	telescope
il televisore	*eel televee**zo**ray*	television
il coltellino	*eel coltel**lee**no*	pocketknife
il tempo	*eel **tem**po*	weather
la tenda	*la **ten**da*	curtain, tent
le tende	*lay **ten**da*	curtains, tent
il tennis	*eel **ten**nees*	tennis
il termometro	*eel tair**mo**maytro*	thermometer
la terra	*la **tair**ra*	earth
la testa	*la **tes**ta*	head
il tetto	*eel **tet**to*	roof
la tigre	*la **tee**gray*	tiger
tirare	*tee**ra**ray*	to pull
il tiro a segno	*eel **tee**ro a **sen**yo*	rifle range
il tiro al cerchietto	*eel **tee**ro al chair**kyet**to*	ring toss
il tiro con l'arco	*eel **tee**ro kon **lar**ko*	archery
il topolino	*eel topo**lee**no*	mouse
il torace	*eel to**ra**chay*	chest
il toro	*eel **to**ro*	bull
la torre di controllo	*la **tor**ray dee kon**trol**lo*	control tower
la torta	*la **tor**ta*	cake, birthday cake
il tosaerba	*eel toza-**air**ba*	lawnmower
la tovaglia	*la to**val**ya*	tablecloth
il trapano	*eel **tra**pano*	drill
il trapezio	*eel tra**pet**syo*	trapeze
i trasporti	*ee tras**por**tee*	transport
il trattore	*eel trat**tor**ay*	tractor
tre	*tray*	three
tredici	***tray**deechee*	thirteen
il trenino	*eel tray**nee**no*	toy train
il trenino dei fantasmi	*eel tray**nee**no day fan**taz**mee*	ghost train
il treno	*eel **tray**no*	train
il treno merci	*eel **tray**no **mair**chee*	goods train
il triangolo	*eel tree**an**golo*	triangle
il triciclo	*eel tree**cheek**lo*	tricycle
la tromba	*la **trom**ba*	trumpet
i trucioli	*ee **troo**chyolee*	shavings
il tubo di gomma	*eel **too**bo dee **gom**ma*	hosepipe
i tuffi	*ee **toof**fee*	diving

U

gli uccelli	*lyee oo**chel**lee*	birds
ultimo	***ool**teemo*	last
undici	***oon**deechee*	eleven
uno	***oo**no*	one
l'uomo (m)	***lwo**mo*	man
le uova	*lay **wo**va*	eggs
l'uovo (m) fritto	***lwo**vo **freet**to*	fried egg
l'uovo (m) sodo	***lwo**vo sodo*	hard-boiled egg
l'uva	***loo**va*	grapes

V

la vacanza	*la va**kan**tsa*	holiday
i vagoni	*ee va**go**nee*	carriages
la valigia	*la va**lee**ja*	suitcase
la vanga	*la **van**ga*	spade
la vasca	*la **vas**ka*	bath
il vassoio	*eel vas**so**yo*	tray
vecchio	***vek**kyo*	old
la vela	*la **vay**la*	sailing
veloce	*vay**lo**chay*	fast
venerdì	*venair**dee***	Friday

venti	***ven**tee*	twenty
il vento	*eel **ven**to*	wind
il verde	*eel **vair**day*	green
la verdura	*la vair**doo**ra*	vegetables
il verme	*eel **vair**may*	worm
la vernice	*la vair**nee**chay*	paint
la vespa	*la **ves**pa*	wasp
la vestaglia	*la ves**tal**ya*	dressing gown
i vestiti	*ee ves**tee**tee*	clothes
il vestito	*eel ves**tee**to*	dress
il veterinario	*eel vetairee**nar**yo*	vet
vicino	*vee**chee**no*	near
la videocassetta	*la veedayokas**set**ta*	video
il vigile urbano	*eel **vee**jeelay oor**ba**no*	policeman (traffic police)
il villaggio	*eel veel**laj**jo*	village
il viola	*eel **vyo**la*	purple
il viso	*eel **vee**zo*	face
il vitello	*eel vee**tel**lo*	calf
le viti	*lay **vee**tee*	screws
vivo	***vee**vo*	alive
il volo libero	*eel **vo**lo **lee**bairo*	hang gliding
i volpacchiotti	*ee volpak**kyot**tee*	fox cubs
la volpe	*la **vol**pay*	fox
vuoto	***vwo**to*	empty

W

il water	*eel **va**tair*	toilet
il windsurf	*eel **ween**sairf*	windsurfing

Y

lo yogurt	*lo **yo**goort*	yoghurt

Z

la zaino	*lo **tsa**-eeno*	backpack
le zampe	*lay **tsam**pay*	paws
la zappa	*la **tsap**pa*	hoe
la zebra	*la **tse**bra*	zebra
la zia	*la **tsee**a*	aunt
lo zio	*lo **tsee**o*	uncle
lo zoo	*lo **tsoo***	zoo
la zucca	*la **tsook**ka*	pumpkin
lo zucchero	*lo **tsook**kairo*	sugar
lo zucchero filato	*lo **tsook**kairo fee**la**to*	candy floss

This edition first published in 2008 by Usborne Publishing Ltd, Usborne House, 83-85 Saffron Hill, London EC1N 8RT, England. www.usborne.com
Copyright © 2002, 1999, 1995, 1983, 1979 Usborne Publishing Ltd.
The name Usborne and the devices are Trade Marks of Usborne Publishing Ltd. All rights reserved. No part of this publication may be reproduced, stored in a retrieval system, or transmitted in any form or by any means, electronic, mechanical, photocopying, recording or otherwise, without the prior permission of the publisher. Printed in China.